THE
LOTUS
SEED

SHERRY GARLAND

THE LOTUS SEED

illustrated by

TATSURO KIUCHI

HARCOURT BRACE JOVANOVICH, PUBLISHERS

San Diego   New York   London

Requests for permission to make copies
of any part of the work should be mailed to:
Permissions Department,
Harcourt Brace Jovanovich, Publishers, 8th Floor,
Orlando, Florida 32887.

Library of Congress Cataloging-in-Publication Data
Garland, Sherry.
The lotus seed/by Sherry Garland;
illustrated by Tatsuro Kiuchi.
p.   cm.
Summary: A young Vietnamese girl saves a lotus seed
and carries it with her everywhere to remember a brave emperor
and the homeland that she has to flee.
ISBN 0-15-249465-0
[1. Vietnam—Fiction. 2. Lotus—Fiction.]   I. Kiuchi, Tatsuro, ill.   II. Title.
PZ7.G18415Lo   1993
[Fic]—dc20   92-2913

First edition
A B C D E
Printed in Singapore

HBJ

The paintings in this book were
done in Winsor & Newton oil and alkyd colors on
Crescent no. 310 cold-press illustration board.
The display type was set in Serlio
by Thompson Type, San Diego, California.
The text type was set in Goudy Village
by Thompson Type, San Diego, California.
Color separations by Bright Arts, Ltd., Singapore
Printed and bound by Tien Wah Press, Singapore
Production supervision by Warren Wallerstein and Ginger Boyer
Designed by Trina Stahl

To Dinh,
who longs to see the lotus blooms
of Vietnam once again
—S. G.

To Muneo, Akiyo, and Lin
—T. K.

My grandmother saw
the emperor cry
the day he lost
his golden dragon throne.

She wanted something
to remember him by,
so she snuck down
to the silent palace,
near the River of Perfumes,
and plucked a seed
from a lotus pod
that rattled
in the Imperial garden.

She hid the seed
in a special place
under the family altar,
wrapped in a piece of silk
from the *ao dai*
she wore that day.
Whenever she felt sad
or lonely,
she took out the seed
and thought of the
brave young emperor.

And when she married
a young man
chosen by her parents,
she carried the seed
inside her pocket
for good luck, long life,
and many children.
When her husband
marched off to war,
she raised her
children alone.

One day bombs fell
all around,
and soldiers
clamored door to door.
She took the time
to grab the seed,
but left her mother-of-pearl
hair combs lying
on the floor.

One terrible day
her family scrambled
into a crowded boat
and set out
on a stormy sea.
Bà watched the mountains
and the waving palms
slowly fade away.
She held the seed
in her shaking fingers
and silently said good-bye.

She arrived in a
strange new land
with blinking lights
and speeding cars
and towering buildings
that scraped the sky
and a language
she didn't understand.

She worked many years,
day and night,
and so did her children
and her sisters
and her cousins, too,
living together
in one big house.

Last summer
my little brother
found the special seed
and asked questions
again and again.
He'd never seen a lotus bloom
or an emperor
on a golden dragon throne.

So one night
he stole the seed
from beneath the family altar
and planted it
in a pool of mud
somewhere near Bà's
onion patch.

Bà cried and cried
when she found out
the seed was gone.
She didn't eat,
she didn't sleep,
and my silly brother
forgot what spot of earth
held the seed.

Then one day in spring
my grandmother shouted,
and we all ran
to the garden
and saw
a beautiful pink lotus
unfurling its petals,
so creamy and soft.

"It is the flower
of life and hope,"
my grandmother said.
"No matter how ugly the mud
or how long the seed lays dormant,
the bloom will be beautiful.
It is the flower
of my country."

When the lotus blossom
faded and turned
into a pod,
Bà gave each of
her grandchildren
a seed
to remember her by,
and she kept one
for herself
to remember the emperor by.

I wrapped my seed
in a piece of silk
and hid it
in a secret place.
Someday I will plant it
and give the seeds
to my own children
and tell them about the day
my grandmother saw
the emperor cry.

AUTHOR'S NOTE

For centuries, emperors ruled Vietnam with absolute power because the people believed they were messengers from heaven and all-wise. One emperor built a magnificent palace on the River of Perfumes in the city of Hue, surrounded by majestic mountains. Modeled after the famous Forbidden City in Peking, China, it was a city within a city, filled with fantastic gardens and orchards and surrounded by lotus-filled moats. Elaborate gates and graceful bridges crossed the moats to the part of Hue where the ordinary citizens lived.

In the late 1800s, France conquered Vietnam and made it into a colony. The French exploited the land and people, and soon the emperors lost their power. The last emperor of Vietnam, Nguyen Vinh Thuy, was born in 1913. When he took the throne at the age of twelve, he became Bao Dai, "Keeper of Greatness." Although he had no real power, Bao Dai was a symbol of Vietnamese heritage and he performed at traditional ceremonies.

Many Vietnamese wanted to be free of French rule and become an independent nation again. So, in 1945, Bao Dai abdicated his throne, handing over his golden seal and golden sword to leaders of the independence movement led by Ho Chi Minh. A bloody war followed, until 1954, when Vietnam defeated the French and won its independence at last.

But Vietnam was still a country in turmoil and soon another war erupted between the north and south. This time the United States helped the southerners. The civil war lasted until 1975, when the south was defeated.

As the conquering northern armies swept down, about one million Vietnamese fled by way of boat. They came from all walks of life—teachers, doctors, merchants, farmers, fishermen— leaving behind their homes, possessions, families, and friends. America became the new home for the majority of Vietnamese refugees.